LITTLE TIM
AND THE
BRAVE SEA CAPTAIN

by

Edward Ardizzone

FRANCES LINCOLN CHILDREN'S BOOKS

JJ
ARDIZZONE
EDWARD

J 6/06

First published by Oxford University Press in 1936
This edition published in Great Britain in 2005 and in the USA in 2006
by Frances Lincoln Children's Books, 4 Torriano Mews,
Torriano Avenue, London NW5 2RZ

www.franceslincoln.com

Distributed in the USA by Publishers Group West

British Library Cataloguing in Publication Data available on request

ISBN 1-84507-456-4

Printed in Belgium

1 3 5 7 9 8 6 4 2

Little Tim lived in a house by the sea.
He wanted very much to be a sailor.

When it was fine he spent the day on the
beach playing in and out of the boats, or
talking to his friend the old boatman, who

taught him how to make the special knots that sailors make and many other things about the sea and ships.

Sometimes Tim would astonish his parents by saying, "That's a Cunarder" or "Look at that barquentine on the port bow."

When it was wet or too cold and rough
to play on the beach, Tim would visit his
old friend, Captain McFee.

The Captain would tell him about his voyages and sometimes give him a sip of his grog, which made Tim want to be a sailor more than ever.

But alas for Tim's hopes. When he asked his mother and father if he could be a sailor, they laughed and said he was much too young, and must wait for years and years until he was grown up. This made Tim very sad.

In fact he was so sad that he resolved, at the first opportunity, to run away to sea.

Now one day, the old boatman told Tim that he was going out in his motor boat to a steamer which was anchored in the bay.

Would Tim like to come, too, and lend him a hand with the boat?
Tim was overjoyed.

The boatman went on to say that the captain of the steamer was an old friend of his, and, as the steamer was about to sail, he wanted to say 'good-bye' to him.

Tim made himself very useful, helping to stow gear into the boat, fill the petrol tank, and make all ready to go to sea.

When this was done, the boatman said "Come, give a shove, my lad," and they both pushed the boat down the shingle beach into the water, then clambered on board, and off they went.

It was a lovely day. The sea was blue, and the little waves danced and sparkled in the sunshine.

Tim got more and more excited as they neared the steamer, as he had never been in one before.

When they arrived alongside they clambered on board.

Tim was left on deck while the boatman went to see the captain, who was in his cabin.

Now Tim had a great

idea. He would hide, and, when the boatman left, not seeing Tim, he would forget all about him.

This is exactly what happened.

Off went the boatman and away went the steamer with Tim on board.

When Tim thought there was no chance of being put on shore he showed himself to a sailor.

"Oi!" said the sailor, "What are you doing on here? Come along with me, my lad, the captain will have something to say to you."

When the captain saw Tim he was furious and said Tim was a stowaway and must be made to work his passage.

So they gave Tim a pail and a scrubbing

brush and made him scrub the deck, which Tim found very hard work. It made his back ache and his fingers sore. He cried quite a lot and wished he had never run away to sea.

Well done my lad

After what seemed hours to Tim, the sailor came and said he could stop work and that he

had not done too badly for a lad of his
size. He then took Tim to the galley where
the cook gave him a mug of cocoa.

Tim felt better after the cocoa, and when the sailor found him a bunk, he climbed in and was soon fast asleep. He was so tired he did not even bother to take off his clothes.

Tim soon got accustomed to life on board. As he was a bright boy and always ready to make himself useful, it was not long before he became popular with the crew. Even the captain said he was not too bad for a stowaway.

Tim's best friend was the cook, who was a family man. Tim would help him peel potatoes, wash up and tidy the galley, and in return the cook would give Tim any nice titbits that were going.

Besides helping the cook, Tim would run errands and do all sorts of odd jobs, such as taking the captain his dinner and the second mate his grog, helping the

man at the wheel and sewing buttons on the sailors' trousers.

One morning the wind began to blow hard and the sea became rough, which made the steamer rock like anything.

At first Tim rather enjoyed this. It excited him to watch the big waves and see the crew hurrying about the deck making everything shipshape and secure.

But alas, Tim soon began to feel sick,

and when he went down to the galley he could not eat any of the titbits that the cook gave him.

All that day it blew harder and harder and the sea became rougher and rougher till by nightfall it was blowing a terrible gale.

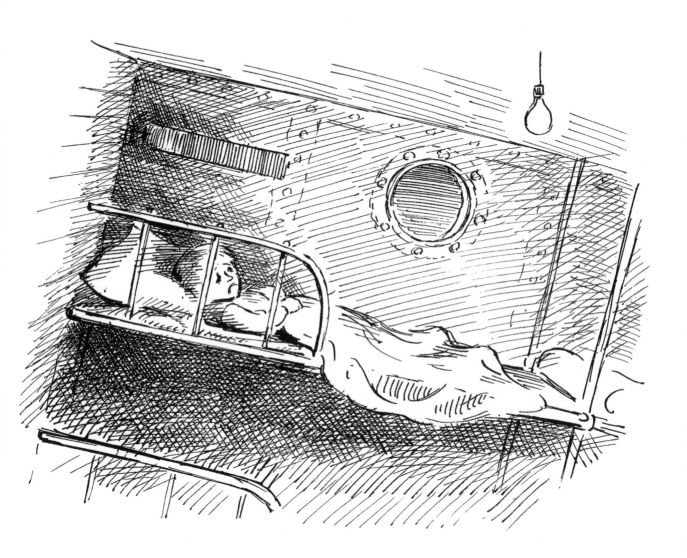

Poor Tim felt so sick that all he could do was to creep into his bunk and lie there, wishing he had never gone to sea.

In the middle of the night there was a
terrible crash. The ship had struck a rock
and lay on its side with the great waves
pouring over it.

The sailors rushed on deck shouting,

"We are sinking. To the boats. To the boats!"
With great difficulty they launched the boats and away they went in the raging sea.

– BUT –

— they had quite forgotten Tim. He was so small and frightened that nobody had noticed him.

Tim crept on to the bridge where he found the captain, who had refused to leave his ship.

"Hullo, my lad," said the captain. "Come, stop crying and be a brave boy. We are bound for Davy Jones's locker and tears won't help us now."

So Tim dried his eyes and tried not to be too frightened. He felt he would not mind going anywhere with the captain, even to Davy Jones's locker.

They stood hand in hand and waited for the end.

Just as they were about to sink beneath
the waves Tim gave a great cry. "We're
saved. We're saved."

He had seen a lifeboat coming to rescue them.

The lifeboat came alongside and a lifeline was thrown to them.

Down the lifeline, first Tim, and then the captain were drawn to safety. But only just in time.

Hardly had they left the steamer when it sank beneath the waves.

Now followed a terrible journey through
the raging sea.

The lifeboat was tossed about like a cork

by the great waves which often dashed over
the side and soaked them to the skin.

It was many hours before they neared land,
and all were very cold and wet and tired.

When the lifeboat came into harbour the crowd, which had gathered on the quay to watch its return, gave a great cheer. They

had seen Tim and the captain and had realized
that the lifeboat had made a gallant rescue.
As soon as the lifeboat had moored beside

the quay, Tim was lifted out and he and the captain were taken to the nearest house.

Here they were wrapped in blankets and sat in front of the fire with their feet in tubs of hot water. Also they were given cups of hot cocoa and so were soon nice and warm, both inside and out.

Once they were warm right through they were put to bed.

They were still very tired from their terrible adventure, so they slept for hours and hours.

When they woke up the next morning, however, they both felt rested and were glad to be alive and well.

Tim hurried to send a telegram to his parents saying he was taking the train home and that the captain was coming too.

Then he and the captain, after thanking the lifeboatmen and the kind people who had put them up, went to the station and caught their train.

On the platform they were surprised to see a large crowd waiting to see them off.

Among the crowd were many ladies who kissed Tim and gave him chocolate and fruit to eat on the journey.

Tim felt very excited and could not help feeling a bit of a hero.

But Tim became even more excited as the train neared his home town.

He had his nose glued to the window all the time looking out for familiar places and pointing them out to the captain when he saw them.

Tim's parents were at the garden gate when they arrived.

Captain McFee and the boatman were there, too.

You can imagine how pleased Tim was
to see his father and mother and his old
friends again.

The captain told Tim's parents all about

their adventures and how brave Tim had been, and he asked them if they would let Tim come with him on his next voyage as he felt that Tim had the makings of a fine sailor.

Tim was very pleased and happy to hear his parents say yes.

The lifeboatmen were pleased, too, as they were presented by the Mayor with medals for bravery.

— THE END —

Presented to
the

**WEST HARTFORD
PUBLIC
LIBRARY**

In Memory Of
Anne Cecere